The Day It Rained Forever

The Day It Rained Forever

About the ONCE UPON AMERICA® Series

Who is affected by the events of history? Not only the famous and powerful. Individuals from every part of society contribute a *story*—and so weave together *history*. Some of the finest storytellers bring their talents to this series of historical fiction, based on careful research and designed specifically for readers ages 7–11. These are tales of young people growing up in a young, dynamic country. Each *ONCE UPON AMERICA* volume shapes the reader's understanding of the people who built America and of his or her own role in our unfolding history. For history is a story that we continue to write, with a chapter for each of us beginning, "Once upon America."

The Day It Rained Forever

A STORY OF THE JOHNSTOWN FLOOD

BY VIRGINIA T. GROSS

ILLUSTRATED BY RONALD HIMLER

PUFFIN BOOKS

Thanks to my husband, Bernie, chauffeur and researcher,
whose endless supply of quarters helped me to copy what
I needed to have.

PUFFIN BOOKS
Published by the Penguin Group
Penguin Books USA Inc., 375 Hudson Street, New York, New York 10014, U.S.A.
Penguin Books Ltd, 27 Wrights Lane, London W8 5TZ, England
Penguin Books Australia Ltd, Ringwood, Victoria, Australia
Penguin Books Canada Ltd, 10 Alcorn Avenue, Toronto, Ontario, Canada M4V 3B2
Penguin Books (N.Z.) Ltd, 182–190 Wairau Road, Auckland 10, New Zealand

Penguin Books Ltd, Registered Offices: Harmondsworth, Middlesex, England

First published in the United States of America by Viking Penguin,
a division of Penguin Books USA Inc., 1991
Published in Puffin Books, 1993

20 19 18

Text copyright © Virginia T. Gross, 1991
Illustrations copyright © Ronald Himler, 1991
All rights reserved

LIBRARY OF CONGRESS CATALOGING-IN-PUBLICATION DATA
Gross, Virginia T.
The day it rained forever: the story of the Johnstown flood / by Virginia T. Gross;
illustrated by Ronald Himler. p. cm. — (Once upon America)
"First published in the United States of America by Viking Penguin . . . 1991"—Verso t. p.
Summary: When a cheaply constructed dam above Johnstown bursts
under the onslaught of torrential rains, Christina and her family
struggle to escape the floodwater which bears down upon their town.
ISBN 0-14-034567-1
1. Floods—Pennsylvania—Johnstown—Juvenile fiction.
[1. Floods—Pennsylvania—Johnstown—Fiction.]
I. Himler, Ronald, ill. II. Title. III. Series.
PZ7.G9043Day 1993 [Fic]—dc20 92-44712 CIP AC

ONCE UPON AMERICA® is a registered trademark of Viking Penguin,
a division of Penguin Books USA Inc.
Printed in the United States of America

In memory of my mother,
Teresa Barille Cartenuto,
who filled my life with stories
of floods and other wonders

Contents

The Warning

"Herbie's It and caught a fit and don't know how to get over it!"

"Gotcha!"

"No, you don't, Herbie! Do *not!*"

From the porch, Christina Berwind listened to her younger brother and sister playing Pinwheel Tag in the barnyard. They had gotten the red, white, and blue pinwheel at the Decoration Day parade in Johnstown that morning.

Christina didn't look up. She didn't want to waste a minute. The linen towel she was stitching was for

Uncle Herbert and his bride, Lenora. Their wedding was in six days!

Papa leaned forward in his rocker. "Margretta! Herbie! Run to the barn and close the loading bay before it rains. Won't do to have the last of our hay soaked before the new crop's in. Better go right now. The sky's looking heavy."

"All right, Papa!" Margretta answered. "You're It, Herbie." Gretta shot toward the barn, followed by the five-year-old.

Isaac Koehler, their neighbor and South Fork's best tobacco chewer, put his hands on his knees and sent a stringy brown spurt toward the spittoon. Christina was thankful his aim was good. Mama didn't allow any spitting in the house, but as soon as the weather turned warm, she put a spittoon on the porch. Mr. Koehler would be coming to visit during the long summer evenings and Mama wanted him to have plenty of room for his tobacco tricks.

"So Teresa stayed in town to help Herb and Lenora get ready for the big day, eh?" he asked.

"She did," said Papa. "Got some fancy bows to tie so each of the wedding guests can take home a favor."

"Well, it's probably good for her to go and get her mind off the young one's death," said Mr. Koehler.

Papa's face turned grim. "Yes. She's taken it pretty hard. You hold the little thing for five minutes and you love it for life."

Even without looking, Christina could see the hill-

side where a small cross marked her sister's grave. The baby had been so little, so helpless. For three terrifying hours, Christina had held it close, listening to its zigzag breathing. She could still feel that last gentle shudder . . . could still feel the warmth passing out of the tiny body. That was two months ago, but the hurt was now.

At the mention of the baby, Frederick got up from the porch steps and moved to the corner of the railing. He looked away at the metal-gray Pennsylvania sky. Christina knew that her big brother kept the roots of his feelings alive, but he also kept them hidden. Frederick was fifteen. In all of her eleven years, she'd never seen him cry.

Mr. Koehler rambled on. "What do you think, George? Looks like this here storm that's coming is going to be a smasher. Wind's circling from the east, too. Don't like that."

Papa glanced toward the barn, waiting for the children to return. The sky was thick with thunderheads. "Can't take too much more rain this spring," he agreed. "The stream's up to its banks now."

"Stream's not what worries me. It's that dam up yonder. I tell you, George, one day that dam's going to bust through, and this valley will be a goner!" Mr. Koehler was working on flooding the spittoon as he spoke.

"Of course, you and me, we don't need to worry," he admitted. "We're sitting pretty up here, but those folk in South Fork and Mineral Point and, why, hey, even Johnstown. Those twelve miles would be nothing once the water reached the Little Conemaugh. There's upwards of twenty million tons of water in that dam."

"But, Mr. Koehler, people always talk about the dam. Look at the rains last year and in 1885. Nothing much happened. Those people in Johnstown always have three feet of water in somebody's cellar from one or the other of those streams. That earthworks at the dam is close to one hundred feet high!"

Christina glanced up. Lately, with Frederick's new deep voice, she couldn't tell whether it was he or Papa speaking. This time it was Frederick.

Mr. Koehler turned toward the boy. "No, it isn't, sonny, ever since the folks at the South Fork Hunting and Fishing Club shaved off the top to make a road." The old man's cheek bulged with each chew. "All those millionaires from Pittsburgh, they wanted their lake and their clubhouse and their summer place. Well, they got what they wanted! A nice deep lake!"

"It's a beauty," Frederick murmured.

"Yes, it surely is that, young man, but let's hope the Beauty doesn't become a Beast. What that lake doesn't have is a single runoff pipe so the dam can be drained if it's close to overflowing." (*Spit, splat!*)

Papa looked surprised. "What do you mean, Isaac? There were five cast-iron pipes sunk in that dam when it was built!"

"Not anymore." Mr. Koehler sniffed. "Didn't know that, hey?"

Frederick swung his feet off the railing. "But when they rebuilt the new dam—"

"They didn't know anything about rebuilding anything. Or if they knew, they didn't want to pay for it. Did they get an engineer to help? No, sir! They got a *muleskinner* to do the work, so he could use his mules and wagons. A *muleskinner!*"

The louder Mr. Koehler talked, the faster he chewed. "The rich got a dandy new lake. And the rest of us got 20 million tons of dammed-up water behind a big old dirt wall." (*Aim, spit. Bull's-eye!*)

Christina poked her needle quickly in and out of the linen. She was bothered by this talk. The huge dam had always seemed like a living thing to her. Often when she walked to where the farm lane joined the mountain road, she would stop and look north. Two miles up-valley, a great wall of earth choked the valley shut. Behind the wall lay Lake Conemaugh, two miles long and 70 feet deep. Below, in the crease between the mountains, South Fork Village looked tiny, almost helpless. Looking at the huge dam made Christina feel tiny and helpless, too. It made her want to reach for something solid, a branch or piece of rock.

Mr. Koehler scowled. "Know what else, George? Now here's something I just found out last week." The old farmer leaned forward, letting his mouth get more

6

juicy than usual. "I was talking with the manager of that place, and he tells me that they've put a grating over the northern spillway to keep the fish in. Isn't that the limit?" He slapped his knee with his fist. "It just isn't right! Those sons of Beelzebub! They think that money gives them the right to do anything!"

Papa stood up. "Isaac, you might want to get along before the bottom falls out of the sky. Looks pretty threatening." It was the cussing, not the weather that got Mr. Berwind to his feet. He was a religious man who kept himself and his family clean-spoken.

Mr. Koehler knew he'd stepped beyond bounds. "I apologize, George. You're right. The storm will soon be starting and old Appomattox here, he doesn't take too kindly to a pelting." He moved toward his horse. "C'mon, old friend, we'll get you home. It's not far," he said, patting the horse's rump.

"Oh, George, say!" said Mr. Koehler as if he'd just remembered something. "Is Teresa coming home soon?"

"Frederick's fetching her tomorrow."

"Do you think if she gets the big iron out one day next week, she could press up my Sunday suit before the wedding?"

Christina smiled up at the squinty old man. "I can do it, Mr. Koehler. Bring it down." It was the first he had looked at Christina all afternoon, she'd been so quiet.

Mr. Koehler's face softened and he touched her cheek with the back of his hand. "I'll bet you can, missy. I'll bet you can!"

The children shrieked around the barn just as the first fat drops began to fall.

"Here she comes," hollered Mr. Koehler, grabbing his horse's reins and leading him in a half-trot down the lane. Appomattox would get a pelting, like it or not!

The Pelting

Frederick walked into the kitchen. He had just come from closing the upstairs shutters against the rain. "It's a good thing we left Johnstown right after the parade, Pa," he said. "We'd have been pushing the wagon behind the team instead of their pulling us if this storm had hit while we were on the road."

Papa, wearing boots and a rubber cape, stood by the porch door. "Are you all right here now, Christina? Can you manage?" he asked.

Christina, wrapped in a white butcher's apron, was slabbing bacon for supper. "I'm fine, Papa," she answered. "If Frederick will just start the stove fire, we can eat as soon as you're back. See? I don't even need Mama!"

Papa laughed and clonked onto the porch. "Milking won't take long," he called back. He started through sheets of rain to the barn.

Raindrops bounced like marbles on the gable. "If this keeps up, I'll have to walk to the city tomorrow," said Frederick. "I'd never take Buggins out in this. It'll take leaving at four to get me to the Iron Works at seven."

Frederick had started his job pitching coal at the Cambria Iron Works the year he finished eighth grade. Christina felt anxious, thinking of him trudging twelve rainy miles to Johnstown. "I'll get up and make you hot farina for breakfast and a good lunch to take," she offered.

Suddenly she stopped slicing and stared at her brother. "If you don't take Buggins, how can you fetch Mama back from Johnstown?" Saying the name of the city made Christina feel loose inside. She wanted her mother home in spite of her brave words to her father.

Frederick saw the worry on his sister's face. "Don't fret," he said. "This will stop. It's raining too hard to last for long."

But it did not stop. During the night, Christina dreamed she was at the parade where drums were beating, beating, only to wake and find it was the rain pounding at the walls. At 4:00, she slipped into her robe and joined Frederick in the kitchen. As she watched him eat his cereal, she thought of the lonely road, and remembered Mr. Koehler's warning about the dam.

"Frederick, don't go today."

"What do you mean? I have to go. It's my work."

"I'm afraid, Frederick. What if Mr. Koehler is right about the dam? What if it burst and you were on the road in the valley? Frederick, stay here." The only light in the kitchen was from the stove fire and from the gas lantern on the table. Christina's eyes looked big and fearful.

Mr. Berwind came into the room. "Tina needs a dose of tonic, Pa. Her imagination is suffering from overwork," laughed Frederick. He turned to his sister. "Listen. Mr. Koehler is an old man who doesn't get to talk to too many people. When he does, his stories get bigger than his good sense."

Frederick looked over Christina's head at his father, waiting for him to agree. Instead, Papa said, "Are you sure they'll be expecting you at work today?"

"Oh, for sure, Pa. I've got to go. I don't want them giving my job to someone else because a little rain kept me away."

Papa looked distracted. Then he said, "All right, but be careful. You'd best plan to stay at Lenora's tonight with your ma. I'll fetch you both in the wagon when I can get there. I've got to say I can't remember a pouring like this, ever."

Wrapped in rubber hood, cape, and boots, Frederick grabbed his miner's pail. In the bottom, Christina had put a lump of ice which would melt into cool water for drinking. In the next layer, she put slices of boiled beef and black bread with horseradish. On top was a large slice of Brown Betty her mother had baked.

At the open back door, the rain noise tumbled about them like thunder and swallowed their goodbyes. Earlier, when Christina had gone out to get cooking water from the rain barrel, it had already filled to overflowing. Now, it couldn't even be seen from the doorway. In two strides, Frederick, too, had become part of the storm.

Christina turned to her father. "I wish Mama were here now," she said. "I wish Frederick could stay home. What if—"

"We'll have no 'what if's,' " said Papa. "Go back to bed now, Tina. When I've milked and fed the animals, I'll make a fireplace fire and we'll all have a good day together waiting for this to pass. I've not had a day off in a coon's age. You and Gretta and Herbie can help me enjoy it. Won't get another any too soon, likely."

Christina didn't want to go upstairs. Like every country kitchen, this one had a couch where family and friends could sit to enjoy good company, or where busy kitchen people could sneak short naps while keeping an eye on dinner. "I'll wait for you here, Papa," she said, settling into the cushions.

"All right, girl. Sleep a bit. The early hour's making you giddy. I'll need you to be rested when those other two wake up." Papa left for his chores.

The old couch hugged Christina like a friend. It smelled of bread baking and wood fires and Mama's naptha soap. It's where Mama sat to darn socks and where she had taught Christina the first words in *McGuffey's Reader*. It was where she, Christina, had hidden marbles and jacks and bounced Herbie when he was a baby and where she had planned to bounce the new baby—Christina stopped short.

The new baby had come and gone, like a summer shower. They had named her Eva. Papa said it was God's will. That she wasn't meant to stay, only to touch their lives long enough to make a difference.

What if it was God's will that Mama or Frederick had finished making a difference and it was time for them to be gone, just like Baby Eva. Panic took her breath away. Papa had said, "No what if's," but she couldn't help herself. Tears squeezed up from deep inside. It was her crying that finally put Christina to sleep—her crying and the rhythm of the rain.

The Bursting

In a small house in Johnstown, Lenora Hastings put the basket of canned plums on the attic steps.

"Whoever thought we'd be spending today moving things from the cellar to the top floor," she said to Christina's mother. "This is one wedding week we'll never forget!"

Teresa Berwind plopped a sack of potatoes next to the plums and caught her breath. "Lenora, I can't figure why Herbert bought you this bungalow so close to the river. He knows the Conemaugh floods every time it rains."

Lenora laughed. Nothing could disturb her today. In one week, she'd be Mrs. Herbert Berwind and all the floodwaters in Pennsylvania couldn't make her sad. "Once we're married, Herbert will be here to help me move things upstairs when the rains come." Her voice glowed like sunshine.

"Well, everything's out of harm's way now, except the parlor carpet," said Teresa. "We'd best gather that up. Should the water come in the house, it would be ruined."

Downstairs again, the two women managed to roll and drag the rug to the stairway. They were struggling to reach the top floor when they heard a spongy gurgle behind them. They turned to see two glassy arms of water spurting through the spaces on either side of the front door near the doorsill.

"Just in time," said Lenora, sounding a little less cheerful. "This is going to mean a barrel of house-cleaning before we can invite 200 guests to a wedding!"

Once in the attic, Teresa hurried to the window. Layers of rain were blowing down the street. Deep water had made yards and sidewalks invisible. Houses were sticking up here and there like rows of well-spaced teeth. "Lenora, come here and look," she called.

In the water-filled street, two men struggled with a flat-bottomed rowboat. One man was bailing out water while the other rowed into the storm. One of the men was Herbert Berwind.

The young man saw Lenora and Teresa and shouted

to them. His words were chopped up by the drumming rain. "Listen!" he yelled. "We're getting everyone out of here to higher land. Stay up where you are. We're getting the downstreet families first! Be back for you as soon as we can!"

"But, Herbert, love . . ." Lenora's protest was tossed away by the wind. She was confused. Johnstown folk had lived through so many floods. The water had never reached an attic before! Why should they leave today?

"I won't be long," Herbert called. The gobbling water fought with the boat as he turned it around. It was shortly before noon.

For the past three hours, Christina had busied herself with house chores and with entertaining Gretta and Herbie, trying to keep her mind off the endless rain. Now, thanks to her efforts, the farm kitchen smelled like fresh bean soup and biscuits.

Outside, the storm showed no mercy. Tender pea plants, the early crop that she and her mother had planted in the kitchen garden, had been driven into the mud. Streamlets of rich garden soil were gushing down the lane.

Papa sat in a corner of the room where he'd fixed himself a small workplace. "Stoke the fire, will you, Tina?" he asked. His hands were filled with wet cane which he was weaving into a new seat for a kitchen chair. "Your ma's been trying to get me to tend to this chore for a month of Sundays. She'll be tickled to see it's done."

Christina shivered with worry at the mention of Mama's name, but she said nothing. Instead, she took a whisk broom and scooped up Herbie. "Herbie, there's more flour on you than in those biscuits. Shall we bake you as well?"

"No, no!" squealed the little boy, as Margretta and Christina pretended to ready him for the oven.

A sudden crashing of footsteps on the porch stopped their play. When the door flew open, Frederick, Mr. Koehler, and a large slice of storm blew into the kitchen.

"Isaac, welcome! Frederick! What are you doing home in the middle of the day?" Papa shouted.

"They shut down the iron works because of high water, Pa. The foreman telegraphed to South Fork and I got the word there. Never did go all the way to the city." Frederick spoke in breathless gulps. "Water's high in South Fork, too. The sheriff grabbed a few of us, asked us to go house to house getting folks to move to higher ground. Pa! They think the dam's going!"

"It's bad, George!" said Mr. Koehler. "I came down to tell you. I was talking with that manager this morning about 11:00. Seems they had eight inches overnight up at the dam. Finally near about 10:00, the lily-livered galoot gave up thinking what the rich folks would say to him about losing their fish and decided it was time to open the spillway. Well, sir, the men couldn't do it. Couldn't do it, I say. The blamed thing was so overgrown with weeds and vines, couldn't get it to budge. Then he ordered about 20 men to start a new channel. The water filled it quick as it got dug!"

Frederick's eyelashes still peaked with rain as he spoke. "About 12:30 a rider came into South Fork with word to telegraph Johnstown and tell them the dam's going to blow. It's terrible, Pa! What're we going to do?"

Christina felt the blood leaving her cheeks. She gaped at her father as he stood, stunned by this news. "Papa?" Her voice was a small thread of sound. Terror pinched into one small unspoken word, the same word that was in the minds of everyone in that room. Her mother's name!

Thinking back, no one could remember whether they first felt the sound or heard it. A simple thunder. A small shaking. But suddenly it was everywhere, each echo louder than the first, rolling and catching itself and exploding against every hillside.

The Berwinds and Mr. Koehler ran down the lane to the edge of the mountain. No one could have imagined this nightmare come to life.

A wall of black water was moving into the narrow valley, tearing up trees and rocks and mixing every-

thing in its path into an angry stew. It passed beneath them with a shuddering force. The village of South Fork flashed in their vision, crumbled into the flood and was gone. The heavy waters picked up speed. On toward Mineral Point, on toward Johnstown.

Only the roaring rain and waves heard Christina's scream. "Mama!"

The Raging

Teresa and Lenora knelt near each other, looking out the attic window. For the past hour, they had not moved. The roaring rain left them with little to say. Outdoors, the crest was high enough to touch. The water lapping at the attic stairs was beginning to push its slow fingers across the wooden floor. Herbert had not returned.

"Teresa?"

"Yes."

"I feel fearful."

"Of course you do, Lenora. This flooding makes me nervous, also."

"I don't feel nervous. I feel, rather, a great dread, as though I'd spoken to Herbert for the last time. That would be worse for me than death, you know."

Teresa took the young girl's hand. "One never knows the future," she said. "Not one moment to the next. But each moment needs to be lived, if we're alive to do it. Some thoughts take life away from the moments we have. It's best not to think them."

Teresa sighed. "You're right," she said, "but still . . . what's that?"

Above the drone of the rain on the roof, the women heard a new, distant sound. Mixed with it was the blasting of a train whistle. It became louder, terrifying, a living, moving thing, replacing the thunder of the rain.

"Teresa, I'm afraid!" Lenora's cry was a shriek against the noise.

"Let us pray together," Teresa said, reaching for Lenora. "Our Father . . ." But as she spoke, an ocean of water smashed through the back wall, tearing Lenora from her arms.

As the house crumbled, the water grabbed Teresa in a death roll, rushing her past roofs and telegraph poles, pulling her under, then spitting her out, only to draw her down again. A piece of roofing gashed against her leg and part of her long skirt was torn away by barbed wire whirling through the flood. A gush of

24

water slammed her into a chimney. She fainted.

When she came to, she was caught in the branches of a giant elm. "Lenora?" she called weakly. "Lenora?" Her words went nowhere. Lenora was nowhere.

Several feet below her, the flood raged and pounded, reaching into the tree to pull her back. She hung on to the stout limbs, fighting for her life. She shut her eyes, too horrified to think.

When she opened them, she saw terrifying things. People, alive and dead, whirling in the waters; animals, pets, furniture, stoves, clothes, all racing by. A book of Shakespeare's poems caught in the fork of some branches. A mattress floated by like a raft, but the woman who had been napping on it when the flood came, lay dead.

Teresa braced herself as an upsurge of water attacked her. When a wooden tub bore down on her like a monster, slamming into her shoulder, she screamed with pain and tried to push it away. It lodged in the branches and wouldn't budge. Its weight was causing them to bend.

She heard it, then. A small cry. A baby's cry! It made no sense to Teresa that a baby should be here in this horror. Still, the baby screamed.

Blinking through a film of dirty water, she saw the howling infant, newborn, wrapped in a soaked blanket and pushed against the side of the tub. She reached for the baby, but she lost her balance. Only the thick branches saved her fall. The tree shook violently,

25

while Teresa, hanging on with one arm, tried to reach the child once more. Another attack from the flood lashed at her, sucking her breath from her lungs. She heard the baby choking. It was useless! Even if she reached it, how long could she hang on to a tree and a baby?

Her mind fogged and her body became slack. *Let the baby go*, she thought. *I'll soon follow it. I'm not afraid to die.* Suddenly she heard a scream. "Mama!" It was Christina's voice. "Mama!" No, she was imagining it, of course. Yet something within her braided her thoughts into a small rope of strength.

She knew what to do. Teresa's heavy apron was still knotted tightly around her waist, its bib looped around the back of her neck. She used her new strength to reach for the tiny form. Lifting the baby out of the tub, she moved it slowly, carefully, across the hissing water. The wet apron bib was stuck to her shirt, but she managed to pull it away and slip the baby behind it. It held the small body against her like a sling.

"There, small one," she sobbed, "we will both be safe—for a while at least." And with her last shred of energy, she pushed the heavy tub out of the tree.

The cobbler, Ronaldo Amici, stood horrified on the hill behind his shop. Squeezing the rain from his mustache and the tears from his eyes, he watched the floodwaters not 20 feet below. Suddenly his attention

27

was caught by movement to his left. Could it be? . . . yes! In the tree . . . a woman.

He ran partway downhill, until he was even with the top of the giant elm. "Madam! Madam!" he called, but the woman's head was slumped forward. Her body was straddling a branch. She was unconscious—or dead. Then he heard the baby's scream.

He could not see the baby, but he knew it was there. Struggling back up the hill, he ran to his shop and gathered rope and a broom. He knew he must hurry.

Tying the rope around his waist, he attached the other end to a tall spruce at the top of the hill. This time he slid down the hill until he was below Teresa. Not five feet below him the flood raged. Underfoot the earth had gone to slog.

He *must* wake the woman. He'd been watching the ebb and flow of the waters. He knew that within minutes a washing wave would reach her again. Maybe she could use the wave to reach him.

"Madam! Madam!" Ronaldo continued to call. Nothing. At the sound of his voice, the baby began shrieking—long, earsplitting screams. It was these needle-sharp sounds that pushed through the darkness of Teresa's mind and made her aware. Her eyes opened.

Tears of relief sprang to Ronaldo's eyes. "Madam!" he screamed. "I can help you."

Teresa was too weak to speak. "This is what you must do," Ronaldo commanded. "Grab the broom.

When the waters rise, let yourself slip from the tree. I will draw you to high ground. Can you do this?"

Teresa nodded yes. Ronaldo was not so sure, but he must try. He lifted the broom to her. The roaring waters told him the time was now. "Hang on for dear life!" he yelled as they were all swept off their feet into the swell.

Gasping, Ronaldo struggled to hang on to the slippery broom handle with one hand and pull himself up the rope with the other. The weight on the broom told him Teresa understood. As they reached the top of the hill, the earth shook and the giant elm, its roots to the sky, was swept away along with the rest.

When Teresa awoke, she was wrapped in a flannel nightshirt and warm blankets.

"Madam will excuse me," said Mr. Amici, "but you were in need of warm clothes. Your own things will dry by the fire." He was feeding the infant a lump of sugar, wrapped in cheesecloth and dipped in warm milk. The baby continued to whimper.

"I fear something is wrong with the baby," said Mr. Amici. "It cries as if it is in pain. When it has been fed, I'll check more closely."

"Are you a doctor?" Teresa's voice was no stronger than a whisper.

"Oh, no," smiled the man. "I live alone, except for the small creatures which come to be fed, and often a bird or a kitten that has been hurt. I've learned from them."

He put the baby on the table and removed the snow-white towels he had used as coverings. He moved his fingers along the baby's neck. As he reached her arm, she screamed out. "Ah, madam, here is the trouble. It can be fixed easily. Your daughter has a broken arm."

Teresa was startled. "She's not my daughter," she said. "She's—I don't know whose she is." The thought of a baby daughter brought Teresa a rush of feeling. She sat up, watching from the couch.

The cobbler put a splint along the baby's arm and tied her arm against her body, so the baby wouldn't move it. Then he brought her to Teresa to hold. It felt good to have the tiny one in her arms. She told Mr. Amici about Baby Eva, about her family at home, about the coming wedding. "I feel certain Lenora is dead." Teresa could say no more.

Mr. Amici listened quietly. "Tomorrow, I will take you home," he said. "The valley road is out of the question, but if you can take some bumps and slides, my horse and buggy knows the high road very well."

The Bringing

After the bursting of the dam, Papa had brought Christina and the terrified smaller children back to the farmhouse. Together with Frederick and Mr. Koehler, they had waited out the rest of the long afternoon. It would take days, perhaps weeks, for the floodwaters to go down. No one knew how long they must wait for news of Mama.

That is why, the next afternoon, when a buggy drove into the lane, they could hardly believe what they saw. Everyone ran to hear what news the driver brought.

A stranger with a black mustache smiled as he moved to help his rider get out.

The rider was Mama.

"Thank God!" Papa cried, racing to his wife.

At the sight of her mother, Christina leaped down the steps but stopped short. Her mother was carrying a baby. Christina froze. Something within her, some secret pain, dropped heavy as a stone.

Mama looked through the smother of shouts and hugs and tenderness at her unsmiling daughter. "Tina," she said. "Come, see."

Christina came closer, staring. It was hard to see through the tears. She hugged Mama with all her might, but was careful to turn her head away. A new baby was something she did not want to see. It was a stranger. Not one of them. What was it doing here?

"I like Mr. Amici's mustache," giggled Herbie.

"I like all of Mr. Amici for saving Mama's life. Do you like him, Tina?" asked Margretta.

"Of course!" Christina scowled.

If had been a whole day since Mr. Amici brought Mama back to the farm and two days since the flood. The three children were on the porch cleaning vegetables for supper. The baby was sleeping in her basket.

"Can I sing to the baby?" It was Herbie.

"She's already asleep," said Margretta.

"And don't wake her up," warned Christina, her voice louder than usual.

"Tina, do you like the baby?"

"Of course I do, Gretta. You're always asking me if I like people! Stop it, will you?"

"You must have a bug in your bloomers, you're so cranky!" Margretta wasn't used to her sister being out of sorts.

"It's just that the baby's too little to like yet," said Christina. "Besides, she's got a broken arm and she doesn't have a name! And we don't even know who she belongs to!"

"Mama says she belongs to us now," said Herbie.

"Well, she doesn't!" snapped his big sister. "At least, not until we're sure there's no kin somewhere." Christina glanced up the hill at the little cross on Eva's grave. It still looked fresh.

"If she does get to belong to us, we could name her Eva," said Margretta.

Christina jumped up, spilling potato peels over her skirt. "No! No! Mama would never name her after our own sister." She turned and ran into the house.

Mama was resting on the kitchen couch. She had offered to finish the linen towels Christina had been sewing for her uncle and aunt's wedding. "We won't throw them away," she had said tearfully. " 'B' is our initial, too. And one day, when it doesn't hurt so much, we'll have a memory." Even Papa had cried.

Now Christina approached her mother, her face flushed and stormy. "Mama, would you name that new baby after our sister, Eva?"

Mama looked at Christina, surprised and puzzled. "Most likely not, Tina."

"Most likely? Yes or no, Mama. Would you?"

Mama stared at Christina for a long minute. "No," she answered softly. "No, we would not."

Christina turned to walk away.

"Tina!" called her mother. "It's not like you to be so rude. What is troubling you?"

Christina tried to bite back a gush of tears, but could not. She buried her face in her mother's lap. "I don't want this baby," she sobbed. "I want my sister."

Mama was quiet for a long time, smoothing Tina's hair, patting her shoulder. Finally she said, "You have your sister."

Tina looked up. She didn't want to play word games with Mama. Mama continued. "Baby Eva was part of you once. That makes her yours forever. The same with this little one with no name. She is part of you now, too. You can choose to love her, or you can choose not. But how you choose makes a difference forever. Can you understand this, Tina?"

"No!" Christina shouted into her mother's skirts. "I don't understand it at all!" The kitchen clock ticked in rhythm with her crying.

At last the girl looked at her mother, her face a mix of tears and guilt. "I think . . . I think, maybe . . . if I try, I could understand it some," she said, wiping her hands across her eyes. "I will try, Mama. But it's so hard."

She got up and started for the porch. At the door, she turned, her breath shaky with leftover tears. "We need to give this baby a name, Mama, a name of her own, just in case . . . just in case she gets to belong to us."

Mama smiled. "We will, Tina. When the time is right, the baby will have a name."

The Naming

Margretta was the first to hear Buggins clomping down the lane. "Frederick's here," she called. "I'll set his place." She put an extra plate, silver, and napkins on the table.

"I didn't expect him back so soon," said Papa. "The way Mr. Amici described things in Johnstown, I thought it would be weeks of working away at the cleanup."

"He's been gone two days, George. Likely he needs a change of clothes and a good tub bath," said Mama.

Frederick appeared at the door, his face and arms

slick with cold water from the pump, his eyes hollow with fatigue.

"What's the news?" asked Papa.

Frederick slumped into a chair. "The count is 2000 dead," he said flatly. "Maybe more. Thousands missing. Looks like no one within blocks of the fork made it through. Hardly a building standing." His words were slow and thick. "Churches, banks, gone. The iron works—destroyed. No food, no water. People stealing." Frederick shook his head, then made himself go on.

"Big trouble happened when the water got to the railroad bridge at the end of town. There was a jam-up 75 feet high. Everything in the water kept piling up against the bridge—furniture and parts of houses and trees and everything. Even bodies.

"At first, folks thought this was a blessing because some of the people began to grab onto things and work their way to dry land. But then . . ." Frederick's voice cracked. "Then, the kerosene and oil in the stoves began exploding and set fire to everything, water and all. And it's still burning!" Frederick lay his forehead in his hand, breathing heavily.

No one spoke.

"They set boards across the pews of a church and all day long, Pa, all day long, we've been bringing bodies there. Digging them out of that burning pile, and sometimes they weren't whole bodies, either." He choked on his words.

Suddenly Frederick stood up, his eyes strange and fiery. "It's all the fault of the greedy rich," he screamed. "Damn them all to hell!"

Except for Mama's gasp, the silence in the kitchen was like a vacuum. Papa stood up. Christina thought he would strike her brother for cursing. Instead, Papa went to the shelf and brought the Bible to the table.

"We best pray," he said, sitting back down. For a long while, the only sound was Frederick's soft moans. Then Papa opened the book and read. "God says, 'Come, you must set your heart right. Then you will forget your sufferings as waters that have passed away. Your life will make a dawn of darkness. You will live secure, full of hope.' Full of hope," he repeated.

"Oh, Pa," Frederick sobbed.

"You'll not need to go back," said his father. "There's lots of ways to help. We'll forge some tools and bring them down. Ma's been baking bread."

Mama's chair scraped as she went to Frederick and helped him to the table. Then, slowly, she went to the corner of the kitchen where the baby was sleeping in her basket. She picked her up and put her in Frederick's arms.

"It is time to name this new life that came to us on the flood," Mama said. She looked directly at Christina. "The baby's name shall be Hope."

The mountain path was muddy and filled with loose

rocks. "Be careful, Gretta!" warned Christina as they picked their way along.

Even in good weather, the walk to school took a long time. The mountain road was always a challenge, but since the flood, it had become dangerous as well.

There had been some talk about not opening school after the flood. Summer vacation was to start soon, anyway. In the end, parents thought it best for the children to have something regular to return to. By June 4th, the little schoolhouse was cleaned and ready for one last week of classes. Now the bell was ringing in its clear, usual way across the valley.

"Let's not be late, Tina. Come on!" Gretta hurried ahead. Their teacher, Miss Rauscher, stood on the porch welcoming her students to the one-room school.

Inside, Margretta took her place on the third grade bench. Christina sat with her sixth grade friends.

After the pledge and Bible reading, Miss Rauscher spoke to the students. "Boys and girls," she said, "this is both a happy and a sad time. Happy because not one of you children was lost in the flood. Sad, because among our friends and relatives in South Fork, 22 children lost their lives." This was the first most of the boys and girls knew of this. Their faces were serious.

"Also," Miss Rauscher continued, "the village school was badly damaged. Two of its walls were knocked away. Because of this, it will not open until

September. We have, indeed, been blessed. Perhaps it is meant that we are to work especially hard during this last week together. With that in mind, let us begin."

No one was ready to begin. Christina could feel Sadie Miller, her friend, trying to get her attention. Sadie scrunched behind her geography book and whispered, "Tell me about the baby at your house."

Christina started to speak. Then she saw Miss Rauscher watching her. "What is it, Christina?" she asked.

"Nothing, ma'am."

"And you, Sadie? You seemed to have something you were most anxious to tell Christina."

"No, ma'am. Well, yes, ma'am. Christina and Margretta have a new baby at their house and I wanted to know about it."

Everyone, including Miss Rauscher, stared at Christina. They all knew about Baby Eva and wondered how this miracle could have happened.

Christina hated being the center of attention. She could feel her ears turning red. Still, she couldn't help but laugh at the amazed looks on everyone's faces. She told the class Hope's story, leaving out the part about her first feelings. She did include the part about how the baby got its name.

Everyone was full of questions.

"Is she yours now?"

"Will she stay with you?"

"Does she have any kin?"

"Does she look like any of you?"

"She doesn't look like nothing right now," chimed in Gretta. "She's bald!"

Everyone laughed. "Doesn't look like *anything*," corrected Miss Rauscher. "What will your family do next, Christina?"

"Well, ma'am, Papa asked Mr. Amici, that's the man who saved Mama, to see what news he could gather in the city. You know, to try to find out if anyone is looking for a small baby. And, well, we're just waiting, that's all."

The Waiting

As spring slipped into summer, it was hard to wait.
Little Hope grew strong and chubby. With her tiny
hands around Christina's fingers, she learned to sit up.
And with her drooly baby smile, she taught the family
to laugh again.

During the heat of August, when Mama spent most
of her time canning tomatoes and beans for winter,
Christina took over caring for Hope, feeding her, bath-
ing her, rocking her to sleep. It was she who noticed
that the baby's first tooth was getting ready to pop

through. After a time, the family seemed to forget that Hope belonged to anyone but them.

It was a dry morning in late summer before they had reason to think about it again. Christina and Margretta were bringing the laundry water to the kitchen when they heard the sound of a buggy wheeling down the lane.

"Mr. Amici," Margretta shouted, dropping her end of the tub. "Mama, come quick."

By the time the little man got out of the buggy, Mama was ringing the dinner bell to call Papa in from the fields. Christina had never paid close attention to Mr. Amici. Now she noticed how small his feet were, how they bounced up the porch steps. She smiled. Everything about him seemed to bounce.

"Tina, our guest might like a cool drink," Mama suggested. Christina found lemonade in the icebox and served it in her grandmother's fine crystal glasses.

"I have news," said Mr. Amici, when everyone had gathered. "News about the baby."

Christina jook tiny breaths, afraid of putting even a small disturbance in the way of Mr. Amici's news.

"As you know, I have been trying to find out all I could about babies lost in the flood. I talked with Mr. John Clarke, a lawyer in the city, explaining everything about the situation. He claims that it would be very hard to prove that this baby belongs to anyone. It is possible she was carried all the way from South

Fork, or from anywhere in between. Most likely, the child's parents have been drowned.

"If someone came looking for the baby, they would have no way of knowing if she were theirs. The baby was only hours old when she was taken by the flood. She has no birthmarks. You would certainly not want to give the child up to someone who might *not* be her true parents."

Mama leaned forward. "Tell us, what does all this mean?"

Mr. Amici smiled. "To quote the lawyer's words, 'There is not a court in the land which would keep the Berwinds from adopting the infant. If they want her, the baby is theirs.' "

Mama and Papa leapt out of their chairs and grabbed the little man's hands. "Forgive our bad manners," laughed Mama, "but we are so overjoyed and so grateful!"

"How can we thank you?" Papa asked.

"May I join you for dinner? It's a long way home and your stew smells delicious. That would be thanks enough." Everyone laughed.

Christina left everyone rejoicing on the porch and slipped into the kitchen. She had just thought of something important that she wanted to do. Hope, still little enough for the basket, was sleeping in her usual corner. Christina lifted her gently and scurried out the back door. "I know you're asleep, Hope, but I must wake you up for this. There's someone who wants to welcome you into the family."

The grasses on the hillside were dry and tickly. The clover, crushed by Christina's footsteps, smelled sweet. As she came closer to the small hillside grave, Christina noticed that it had lost its fresh-dug look, and that the periwinkle she had planted to cover it was thick and green. She sat down and moved the baby into the shade of her body.

As Christina sat thinking about the two babies, she was surprised at how peaceful she felt. "I want you two to get to know each other," she said softly. "After all, you are sisters now."

She felt a cool shadow on her back. "Mama!" Tina jumped up, anxious that her mother might be worried to find Hope gone. "I was just introducing Eva and Hope to each other."

"I thought you might be up here," Mama smiled. "It was a wonderful, thoughtful thing to do, Tina. You did it for us all. Thank you."

Together, the three went down the hill. Mama was humming, Christina was smelling the stew, and Hope was sound asleep.

ABOUT THIS BOOK

As a little girl, I heard my mother tell about the Johns-town Flood. It's something I've always known about. The truth is, I only *thought* I knew about it.

In the spring of 1989, exactly 100 years after the flood, I read about Elsie Frum. Elsie was a child living north of Johnstown when the flood took place. Her story made me realize that real people lived through this disaster. Families, aunts, uncles, children. I de-cided to find out more. Maybe there'd be a story to tell.

The Library of Congress in Washington, D. C., has copies of newspapers, saved on film. They are filled with reports of the flood.

I learned that Johnstown, in western Pennsylvania, often flooded. It sat in a valley where two rivers, Stony Creek and Conemaugh, came together. Most of its 12,000 people worked in iron and steel mills. They never got excited about high water. They knew about the South Fork Dam, 12 miles to the north, and joked about its giving way.

What they did not know was that the dam was poorly built. The millionaires who formed the South Fork Hunting and Fishing Club took shortcuts to save money. Only a wall of earth held back the lake behind the dam. The lake was 70 feet deep. When the rains of May 31st flooded the dam, the earth gave way all at once. One news report said a wall of water 125 feet high rushed down the valley at 50 miles an hour. No one was ready for this.

The sudden force of the water caused horrible things to happen. It became impossible to count lives lost. Some said 2,500, others 7,000. But many who survived became heroes in their own way.

Workers came from all over the country. It took them three months to clear things away and bury the dead. Organizations sent food and clothing. Clara Barton, the 67-year-old founder of the American Red Cross, arrived five days after the flood and stayed for five months. The environment was ruined. Disease was everywhere. It was five years before the iron and steel mills were operating as they once had.

Those who survived survived two things—the flood, and the time after the flood. Reading about these courageous people, it's not hard to believe that a family like the Berwinds really lived.

V.T.G.